Mrs. Leary's

A Legend of Chicago#

C. C. Hine

Alpha Editions

This edition published in 2023

ISBN : 9789357950473

Design and Setting By
Alpha Editions
www.alphaedis.com
Email - info@alphaedis.com

Contents

"ORIGIN OF THE CHICAGO FIRE.

"On the other side of this card will be found a life-like picture of Mrs. Leary and the cow that kicked over the lamp that caused the great fire in Chicago.

"Mrs. Leary got her living by selling milk; she had five cows, and kept them in her barn on De Koven street, on the west side of the river. A neighbor woman called on her for a pint of milk at nine o'clock Sunday night, October 8th, and Mrs. Leary, having sold all she had, went to the barn with her lamp to make a further draft on her best cow. The cow, as seen by the picture, being a spirited animal, became indignant at the attempt, kicked over the lamp, setting the barn on fire, and thus inaugurated the greatest fire the world has ever seen."]

MRS. LEARY'S COW.

THIS is the Cow, at the Leary back gate,
Where she stood on the night of October the 8,

With her old crumpled horn and belligerent hoof,
Warning all "neighbor women" to keep well aloof.
Ah! this is the cow with the crumpled horn
That kicked over the lamp that set fire to the barn
That caused the Great Fire in Chicago!

THIS is Chicago, all blasted and burned,

The Paradise whither insurance men turned;

But from which they now bring sad faces away,

Sorely vexed with the losses they're called on to pay,

Since the fire-fiend encircled the city that day.

And they swear at the cow with the crumpled horn

That kicked over the lamp that set fire to the barn

That caused the Great Fire in Chicago!

THE FIRE FIEND ENCIRCLED THE CITY.

THIS is the Frame Range of best northern pine,

The banquet on which hungry flames love to dine,

Which agents so oft manage *not* to decline,

But write (in their slop-bowls) a "moderate line,"

Because—don't you see—the commish is so fine.

THE FRAME RANGE.

Ha! this is the range which delighted to carry

The passenger flames o'er the devil's own ferry,

And utilize mischief by spreading it faster

Than men could compete with the fearful disaster.

How sad and how strange are the memories now

Which hang round the heels of that old Leary cow—

That wretched old cow with the crumpled horn

That kicked over the lamp that set fire to the barn

That caused the Great Fire in Chicago!

THIS is the Company, gloomy and glum,

Which admits that it has some few (?) losses, yes *some!*

But its officers think their best motto is "mum,"

As they stroke their gray chins and look wise and sing dumb;

THE COMPANY GLOOMY AND GLUM.

While inside they are praying, "Good Lord, please deliver

Our souls from the fear of old Miller's receiver."

And they view with the most acrimonious hate

That regurgitant cow at O'Leary's back gate,

As she stood on the night of October the 8,

When she kicked at the lamp that set fire to the barn

That caused the Great Fire in Chicago!

THIS is the Statement the Company made:

(Directors and Officers thickly arrayed,

To soften the jar as they strike the up grade,

Where the millions of losses will have to be paid.)

"Our agency records, we deeply regret,

Are burned at Chicago, are out in the wet,

Or else there is, h—m, there is some slight impediment,

Some something-or-other, some sand or some sediment

Has got in the keyhole, disordered the lock,

Or razeed the dividends, watered the stock,

Or some trifling thing not yet quite in sight;

But the *Company*, sir, is all right, is all right;

THE STATEMENT THE COMPANY MADE.

Our surplus is safe, and our stock is intact,

Our losses are all reinsured—why, in fact,

We never, in all our official career,

Felt more gay and festive, more full of good cheer.

Just put up the rates and go on with the biz,

These losses will all be arranged with a whiz.

The thing we will have straightened out in a jiffy,

And the next that you'll hear will be ten per cent, divvy."

But you ought to have seen them when, in the back room,

They poured out anathemas like a mill-flume

On that old Leary cow with the crumpled horn

That kicked over the lamp that set fire to the barn

That caused the Great Fire in Chicago!

———————————————————

IN THE BACK ROOM.

THIS is November, a month from the fire;

And the ascertained losses reach higher and higher.

As the figures go up the long faces go down,

Till the month-ago-boaster appears like a clown.

The trick of deception is voted a sham;

The people say *fraud*, and the agents say —————,

And the grim old receivers call round for the keys,

The assets, the papers, the books, if you please.

AND SQUEEZE HIMSELF THROUGH THE SMALL END OF A HORN.

Of all unwelcome things that this world ever saw,
The bitterest is a compulsory *craw*.
For a large-swelling dignity, proud and high born,
Who claims that his status is bright as the morn,
To get down and meekly acknowledge the corn,
And squeeze himself through the small end of a horn,
Suggests that a little less premature crowing,
A little more system, a little more knowing,

Some better kept books and more accurate showing,

Are best, in the long run, for our underwriters,

To save them the sneers and the jeers of backbiters,

The scoffs of the public, the quips of the writers,

And a toss from the cow with the crumpled horn

That kicked over the lamp that set fire to the barn

That caused the Great Fire in Chicago!

THE CLAIMANT SO PURE AND SO MILD.

THIS is the Claimant, so pure and so mild,

With his heart and his manners as bland as a child,

Whose amiability never is riled,

And whose modest demands with his loss proofs are filed.

His property cost, as he shows from his deeds,

A sum which ten thousand times over exceeds

The mite of insurance for which he now pleads.

His goods, to be sure, they were mostly sold out;

His building within was a shell, and without

Was veneered with cheap stone, or thin iron, or grout;

But *his word*, bless my soul! who could harbor a doubt,

Its truthfulness or its exactness about?

So he pockets his funds, and he rolls up his eyes,

This mild-mannered man, with a cheerful surprise;

And he rubs his two hands with an innocent glee,

Which would do, I am sure, your heart good for to see,

As he *blesses* the cow with the crumpled horn

That kicked over the lamp that set fire to the barn

That caused the Great Fire in Chicago!

THIS is an Adjuster! Now open your eyes.

A man who the trade of rapacity plies!

AN ADJUSTER, (AS THE CLAIMANT REGARDS HIM.)

He will cut down your claims, he will cut up your proofs,

He will riddle your case through its warps and its woofs.

And search all your houses from cellars to roofs

For a sliver by which he may fasten a quibble

And curtail your claim to a bite or a nibble.

And then when you think he is ready for payment

He will make you regret you were ever a claimant,

By charging you discount for those sixty days,

Or vexing you further with needless delays.

These awful adjusters! they should be ashamed

To ply a vocation so loudly defamed.

AS HE REGARDS HIMSELF—A MUCH ABUSED INDIVIDUAL.

"What's the good of insurance if not to pay losses?

And why all these questions, and bothers and crosses?

And why are we hampered and why are we checked?

Insurers can claim (if you'll only reflect)

No rights which it is not *our* right to reject;

No rights which the people are bound to respect.

They must smile and be patient, and out with their purses,

And take what we give them, our kicks or our curses;

Bow down to the cow with the old crumpled horn

That kicked over the lamp that set fire to the barn

That caused the Great Fire in Chicago!"

THIS is Insurance. Now, satire, farewell!

For the woes which the fire-stricken city befel,

Must have rung like the clang of a destiny knell,

RELIEF IN HER HANDS AND DELIGHT ON HER WINGS.

Through the years of prostration and clog and delay,

Which would drag unsupportable all the sad way,

Through which her redemption and rising must lay,

Had Insurance not sped, like an angel that brings

Relief in her hands and delight on her wings.

All honor we give to the craft that we love;

It has for its motto the word from above;

The word spoken erst by omnipotent love.

The burdens of each in Insurance we bear,

And its benefits all its participants share.